Norman Didn't Do It!

(Yes, he did.)

BY RYAN T. HIGGINS

DISNEY · HYPERION

Los Angeles   New York

For my accomplice, Tracey Keevan,
who shall remain nameless

Text and illustrations copyright © 2021 by Ryan T. Higgins

First Edition, September 2021
10 9 8 7 6 5 4 3 2
FAC-034274-21350
Printed in the United States of America

This book is set in Macarons/Fontspring with hand-lettering by Ryan T. Higgins
Designed by Tyler Nevins
Illustrations were created digitally

Library of Congress Cataloging-in-Publication Control Number: 2020046343
ISBN 978-1-368-02623-9
Reinforced binding
Visit www.DisneyBooks.com

Norman was a porcupine.

Norman's best friend was Mildred.

Mildred was a tree.

Norman and Mildred did everything together.

Norman was happy with the way things were.

Okay. One more chapter. Then it's lights-out, Mildred.

Norman and Mildred.

Mildred and Norman.

Just the
two of them.

Until one day . . .

POP!

there was someone else.

It was another tree.

Suddenly, it was no longer just Norman and Mildred.

Now it was Norman and Mildred and *the other tree.*

This did not sit well with Norman.

Norman began to worry.

What if the other tree wanted
to be friends with Mildred?

What if Mildred LIKED the other tree?

What if Mildred liked
the other tree MORE
than she liked Norman?!

Norman kept a careful eye on the other tree.

WHOOOSH

He watched as Mildred and the other tree grew closer.

BOUNCE

BOUNCE

Then it happened.
The worst thing possible.

Mildred and the other tree grew TOO close together.

It was the last straw.

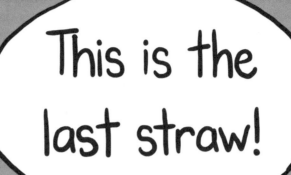

This is the last straw!

Even though, in this case,
there were no straws.
Just branches.

Norman could not lose his best friend.
Not to *the other tree*.

Something had to be done.

Norman planned and he planned
until his plan was just right.

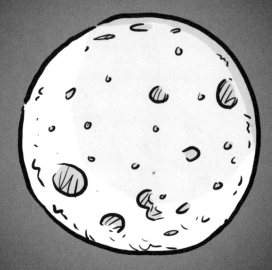

Then, under the cover of night,
Norman dug up the other tree.

And took it
far away.

Very far away.

Very, very far away.

To a place where the other tree would never come between Norman and Mildred ever again.

And just like that, the other tree was gone.

Norman and Mildred
were back together.

Just the two of them.

But it wasn't the same.

Soon, Norman started to think about Mildred— without her new friend.

Norman started to think about the other tree— all alone out there.

Norman started to think about himself— and what he did.

What if someone had seen him?

What if digging up your friend's friend
in the middle of the night
and taking that friend very, very far away
was NOT the right thing to do?
What if it was the WRONG thing to do?

Norman had hit rock bottom.

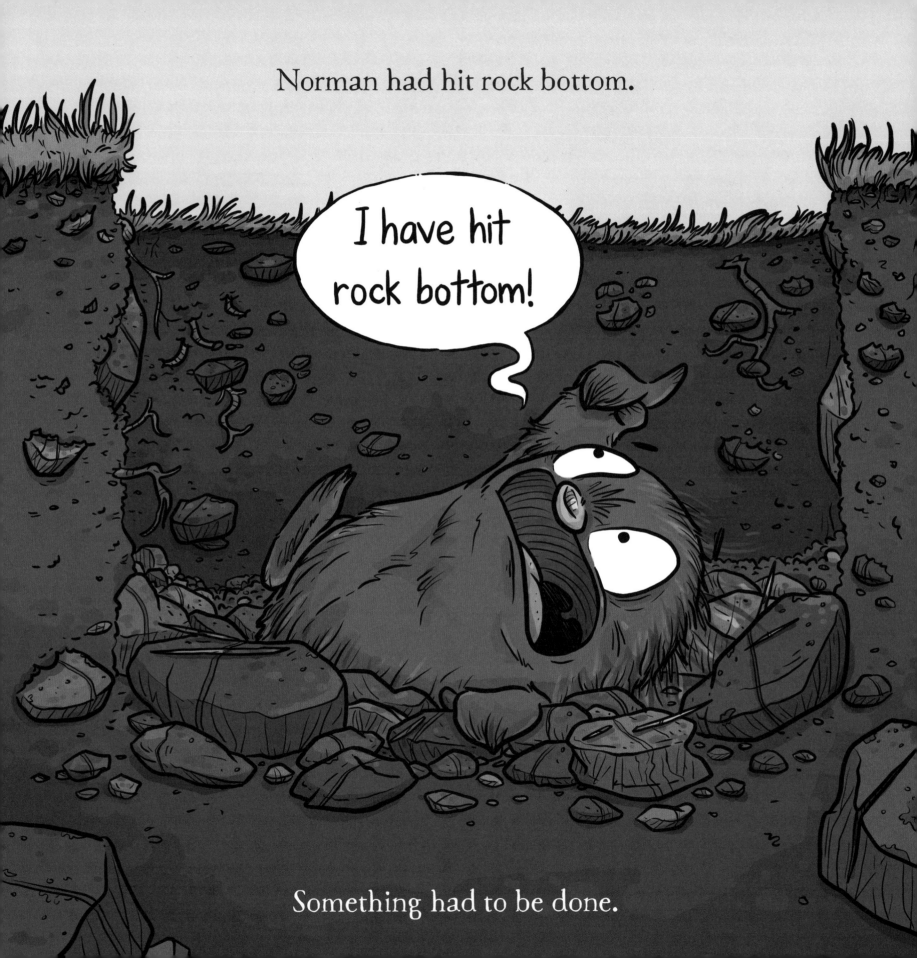

Something had to be done.

Norman planned and he planned. Again.

Then he went back . . .

to where he had left
the other tree . . .

. . . to try and undo what he had done.

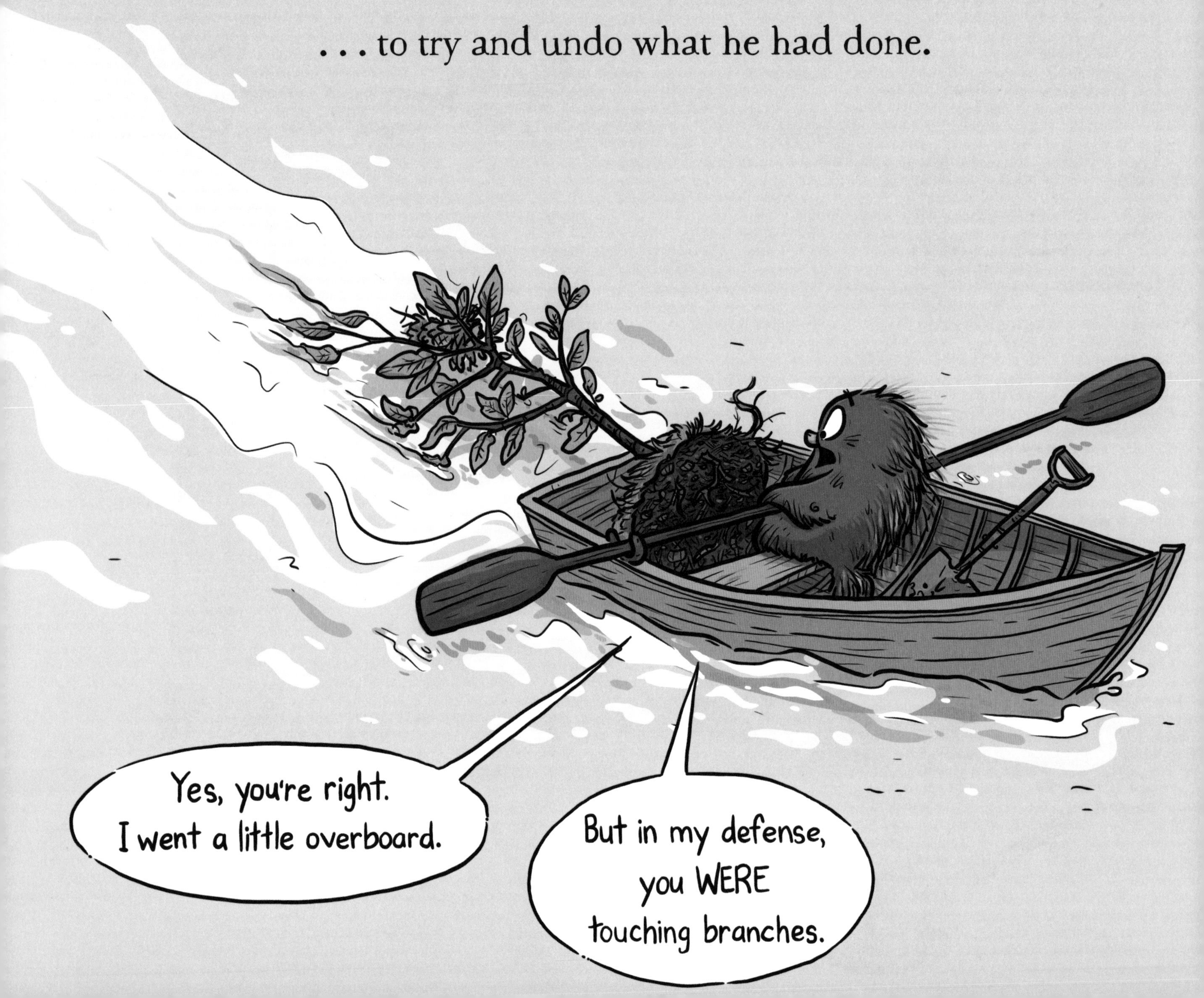

Norman knew life was
going to be different.

And that was okay.

He might even like it.

Norman . . . and Mildred . . .
and the other tree.

Just the three of them.